BALARIN'S GOAT

STORY AND PICTURES BY

HAROLD BERSON

CROWN PUBLISHERS, INC., NEW YORK

Also by Harold Berson

HOW THE DEVIL GETS HIS DUE

Printed in the United States of America
Library of Congress Catalog Card Number: 72-79795
ISBN: 0-517-50068X
ISBN: 0-517-501058
Published simultaneously in Canada
by General Publishing Company Limited
First Printing

The text of this book is set in Egmont
The illustrations are 3/color pre-separated ink
and wash drawings with wash overlays,
reproduced in halftone.

BALARIN'S GOAT

Once there was a farmer named Balarin
who had a wife named Marinette. They lived
on a farm with their pigs, chickens, and
a goat named Fleurette.

Balarin let Fleurette do exactly as she pleased,

whether it was nibbling the vegetables
in the garden,

or chasing the pigs around the barnyard,

or chewing the laundry Marinette had hung out to dry.

Nothing was too good
for Fleurette. Balarin
fed her the finest
delicacies he could find.

He scratched her nose,

hugged her,

and even crowned her
with wreaths of flowers.

But with Marinette it was always,
"Why are you downstairs when
you should be upstairs?"

"Why are you coming when
you should be going?"

"Why are you sitting when you should be standing?"

And on,

and on,

and on.

Marinette grew more and more disgusted.
"Fleurette is treated better than I am," she said.
"One old goat deserves another."

The next day when Balarin returned home
from the fields, he snarled, "What's for dinner?"
"B-A-A-A-A," answered Marinette.

Marinette B-A-A-A-A-ED
while washing,

B-A-A-A-A-ED
while sweeping,

B-A-A-A-A-ED
while spinning,

B-A-A-A-A-ED
while baking.

At last Balarin began to worry.

That night Balarin had a bad dream.

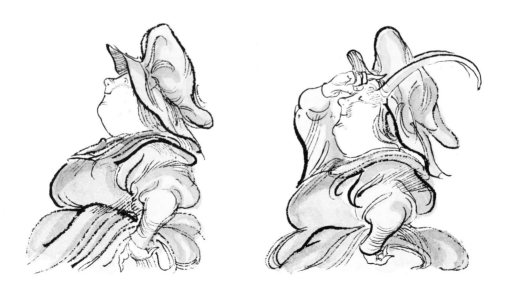

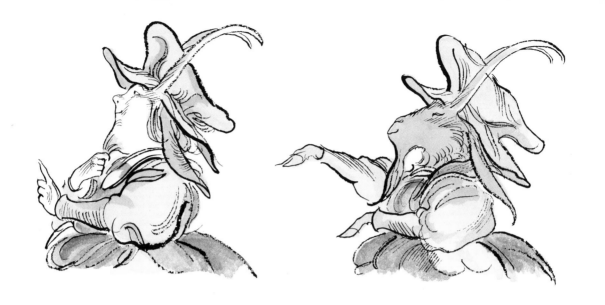

He dreamed that Marinette
had turned into a goat.

In his dream other men went to church with their well-dressed wives. Balarin went to church with his well-dressed goat.

And at market, while other women bargained for
fruits and vegetables, Balarin's wife nibbled them.

As Balarin lay in
his bed, he felt
a kiss on his hand.
"M-m-m-m," he sighed.

Then he felt a kiss
on his face.
"You're too good
to me," he said.

Balarin turned over and reached for
Marinette, but it was not Marinette
he found. It was Fleurette.

Balarin jumped out of bed and
ran through the house calling,

"Marinette, Marinette. Where are you?"
"B-A-A-A," came a reply from the goat house.

Balarin ran across the yard.

"This has gone too far," complained Balarin.
"You belong in the house."
"B-A-A-A," said Marinette.
She lowered her head to butt him.
"Please," coaxed Balarin,
"no more. Won't you come home?"

Marinette put her hands on her hips.
"I will come home, dear Balarin, when you can be
kind, and patient, and cheerful.

And you may start by hugging me,

and kissing me,

and crowning me with wreaths of flowers.

And so Balarin hugged
her, and kissed her,

and crowned her with
wreaths of flowers.

He scratched her nose,

and fed her the finest
delicacies he could find.

And Marinette even saved a few for Fleurette.